Hugs for Mummy

BONNEY PRESS

Published by Bonney Press
an imprint of Hinkler Books Pty Ltd
45–55 Fairchild Street
Heatherton Victoria 3202 Australia
www.hinkler.com

BONNEY
PRESS

© Hinkler Books Pty Ltd 2017, 2018

Author: Louise Coulthard
Illustrator: P.S. Brooks

ISBN: 978 1 4889 1142 2

Printed and bound in China

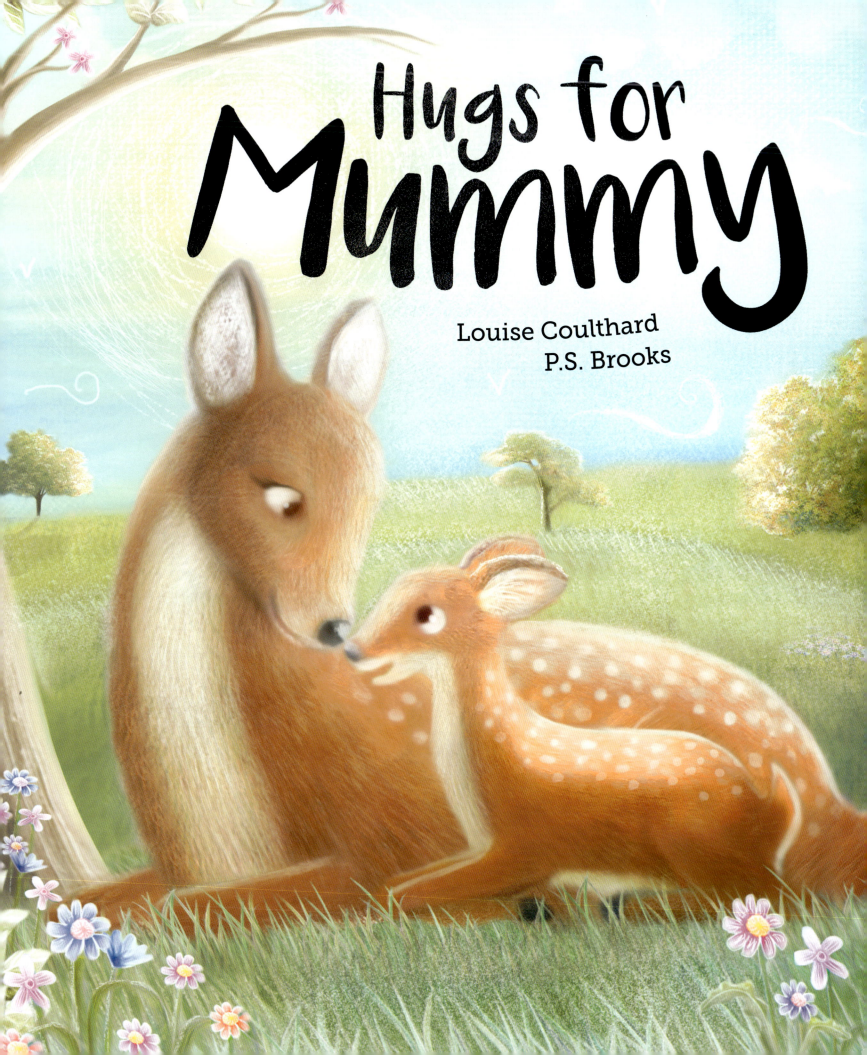

Hugs for Mummy

Louise Coulthard

P.S. Brooks

Mummy, I love you. I feel so precious and special when you hug and hold me tight!

Mummy, as we start each day, you teach me to be curious about the world.

We go exploring and make wonderful discoveries!

Mummy, you find the tastiest treats when my tummy starts to rumble. Thank you for always leaving the yummiest pieces for me!

Mummy, I love the fun we have when I run and leap and dash as fast as I can. You cheer me along and squeeze me tight when I stop for a cuddle.

Watch how high I can jump!

Mummy, you support me when I stumble and help me up when I fall. Oops!

Your hugs teach me that it's okay to make
mistakes and your snuggles help me to try again.

Mummy, we always take time to smell the flowers.

You show me how little moments of beauty can make every day special!

Mummy, you reassure me when I am feeling shy.
Things don't feel as scary when you hold me close.

Suddenly I feel brave enough to try anything!

Mummy, we play the best games together.

I love playing hide and seek with you and it's just as much fun to cuddle when you find me!

Mummy, you show me how wonderful it is that we are all different and that everyone's stories and feelings are important.

Mummy, I love it when we splish and splash together in the river.

I feel safe as we swim side-by-side through the clear water.

Mummy, it's so lovely and safe and warm when we snuggle up tight as you tell me the most magical bedtime stories.

Mummy, your hugs are so special!
But do you know what my favourite hug is?

When it's my turn to hug you back!

I love you **Mummy!**